A **SporTellers**™ Book

STROKE OF LUCK

CHRISTOPHER RANSOM MILLER

CHILDRENS PRESS, CHICAGO

SporTellers™

Catch the Sun
Fear on Ice
Foul Play
High Escape
Play-Off
Race to Win
Strike Two
Stroke of Luck

Childrens Press Edition

Senior development editor: Christopher Ransom Miller
Content editor: Carol B. Whiteley
Production editor: Mary McClellan
Design manager: Eleanor Mennick
Illustrator: Bob Haydock
Cover: Bob Haydock

ISBN 0-516-02268-7

Library of Congress Catalog Card Number: 80–82989
Printed in the United States of America.
1.9 8 7 6 5 4 3 2 1

Contents

CHAPTER 1
The Fish

The race was over. Jeff Nakamura hung on to the pool wall. He felt too tired to pull himself up and out. As he closed his eyes, he felt as if he were going to be sick.

"Good try," a voice above him said.

Jeff forced his eyes open and looked right into a pair of bright blue shoes. They belonged to a man with a whistle. The word *coach* stretched in red letters across the front of the man's shirt.

"That was much better, Jeff," the coach said as he looked down. "But it's still not good enough."

"How much?" Jeff asked. He was too tired to say any more.

"Seconds," the coach said. He shook his head. "You still need to take several seconds off your time."

"I can do it," Jeff said.

The coach smiled at Jeff's words. He had heard them many times before. "Right," he said. He held out a large hand to help Jeff out of the pool. "You'll have to work hard, though."

He handed Jeff a towel as the young man came up to stand next to him. Jeff was thin and tall—more than a head taller than the coach. The coach had to look up at him as he spoke.

"Call it a day, Jeff. The trials are still a long way off."

"Sure thing, Coach," Jeff answered. He knew that it was still 10 weeks until the Olympic trials would take place. They would be held at Los Alamos this year—the pool where Jeff had been training for the last few weeks and where his brother Andy had set so many records. Jeff thought about the trials as he ran a towel over his hair. "We can work more on the 1500 tomorrow, right?"

"Right," the coach told him. But as he spoke, the coach walked away from Jeff. The whistle was in his mouth. "All right, Mike, Carlos," he yelled around the whistle. "On the blocks."

There was the sound of wet feet on concrete. Then quiet. The whistle screamed. There was a splash.

Jeff banged through the door and into the hall. His arms and legs felt dead. The 1500-meter was a long race—almost a mile. His body was still hot from the swim. More than anything, he needed a drink of water.

But someone was already at the water fountain—a short guy in a red sweatsuit. Must be a new swimmer I haven't met yet, he thought.

Jeff rested against the wall. He waited for what seemed like a week. He was so thirsty he felt like an old car on a hot summer day. But the person in the red sweatsuit just kept drinking from the water fountain.

Soon Jeff couldn't wait anymore. He tapped the man on the back. Nothing happened. He tapped again, harder.

"Hey," Jeff said sharply. "Other people want a drink too, you know."

Two members of the women's swim team came up behind him in line as he waited for the man to move. But the man didn't move. Jeff couldn't understand why.

"Listen, guy," he said at last. The women behind him started to laugh. That made Jeff even more angry. He grabbed the red shirt by the arm and started to turn the man around.

"Get your hands off me!" the voice said, catching Jeff by surprise. It sounded different from the way he had thought it would. "And who do you think you're calling a guy?"

Jeff found himself looking into the angry face of a young woman. Quickly he dropped her arm.

"Oh," he said. "I'm sorry."

But the woman in the red sweatsuit just shook her head. She pushed her way past Jeff and then past the other women. Shaking his own head, Jeff leaned down into the cool water of the fountain. As he drank, he heard a voice behind him call down the hall: "Way to go, Fish! You really told that clown off!"

Jeff felt a sharp finger tap him on the back. Then he heard his own words being said by someone else.

"Listen, guy. Other people want a drink too, you know."

When he turned around, Jeff found that the sharp finger belonged to a young woman with dark hair and dark eyes. Jeff could tell that she didn't like him. There was a smile on her face, but it wasn't a friendly smile. He decided to ask her a question anyway. "Who was that?"

"Don't you know anything?" the woman said. "That's the Fish."

"The Fish." Jeff looked back at the woman with a blank look on his face. The words had no meaning for him.

"Jan Fisher," the woman told him. "She's only the best swimmer in the country!"

* * *

Jeff slipped through the door to Pool Number Two. He stood against the back wall and waited for the race to begin. It was a 100-meter freestyle—just down to the end of the pool and back. There were three women on the starting blocks. The one in the middle was the woman who had been wearing the red sweatsuit. She was wearing a red swimsuit now and a red cap over her hair. She looked strong.

In a moment Jeff heard a voice. It sounded high and funny—as if it were coming out of a tin can.

"Women—on your marks!"

The race was about to start.

CHAPTER 2
Viva, Fish!

When Jan Fisher heard Coach Meg Hooper's voice call to her and the other swimmers on the blocks, she moved her body forward and down. Bending her knees just a bit, she stretched her arms behind her like long wings. Then the starting whistle sounded. Quickly Jan used her wings to carry her into the air—out over the blue water of the pool and then down. Her body cut into the water.

She came up swimming fast. Again and again her arms curved down into the water and pulled her along. Her legs kicked hard. They pounded the water into small white bubbles.

She reached the far end of the pool and went into a flip turn. She pulled her head down and under. She folded her legs against her chest.

Around she went. Her toes touched the pool
wall. Then she pushed off, exploding back
down the middle lane as if she had been fired
from a gun. She reached the starting end of
the pool and climbed out long before the other
two swimmers finished.

Jan looked around for Coach Hooper, who
had the stopwatch. But Coach Hooper was at
the back door. She was showing some man the
way out. Coach Hooper didn't like anyone
watching her tightly run practice.

"Was that a friend of yours?" Hooper asked
Jan when she came back. Her tin-can voice
sounded angry.

"I couldn't really see him," Jan answered. "But I'm sure he wasn't. Why? Did he say he knew me?"

Coach Hooper gave Jan a funny look. "He said he was a friend of yours."

"Well, he isn't," Jan said sharply. "I don't have time for friends. Let's forget him. How did I do in the 100?"

"You did fine," Hooper said. She reset her stopwatch. "It's not official, but if that had been an official race, you would have set a new world's record for 100 meters."

Slowly Jan's face softened into a small smile. "I thought it was pretty fast."

"You should do very well at the Olympic trials," Hooper went on. "Just keep your mind on swimming."

"You don't have to worry about that," Jan told her. "My mind is always on swimming."

"Worry about what, Fish?" It was a short woman—the same one who had been hard on Jeff near the water fountain. She had come in from the hall and had just walked up to the pool.

"Nothing, Marty," Jan said. "Coach Hooper's just worried about some guy who was hanging around."

Marty laughed. "Everyone should be hanging around to see the best swimmer on the team—the Fish! Maybe it was a reporter who wants to do a story on you."

Jan just made a face, but Coach Hooper thought Marty might be right. "He probably was a reporter," she said. "But I still don't like people hanging around my swimmers during practice—not without checking with me first." She walked off calling to some other women.

Jan watched her coach walk away. Meg Hooper could be hard to work with, but she was the best there was. People came from all over the country to train with the coaches at Los Alamos, and most of them came to train with Meg Hooper. Jan had come to the Los Alamos Swim Club more than a year ago to train with her, and Hooper had helped Jan a lot. Now Jan's past life in Kansas seemed very far away.

"Come back to earth," Marty Perez said, bringing Jan out of her thoughts. "A group of us is going for pizza. Why don't you come?"

"No I can't, Marty."

"Come on, Fish. I'm always telling the others how great you are. Come with us and show them yourself."

"No thanks," Jan said again. "Some other time."

"Why not now? You need to have fun some of the time. Just dinner. You'll be home early."

"All right. OK. But I'll meet you there," Jan finally said. "I've got to swim a few more laps."

"OK," Marty said. She looked at her watch. "It's almost 5:30. We'll meet you at Sal's Pizza House at 6:30."

Jan's eyes stayed on Marty's back as the shorter woman walked away. She was looking at Marty, but she really didn't see her. Her mind was already on the pool. She had just swum a 100-meter freestyle, but now she was thinking about the 1500-meter freestyle. The two were very different races, but she was going to swim both of them in the Olympic trials. She knew that she had the speed for the 100-meter race. But the 1500-meter race took something more from a swimmer. You had to swim for a long time without getting tired.

Jan climbed onto the starting block. She would swim a practice 1500 meters. In her head, she heard again the cheers of the people in Mexico City.

"Fish! Fish!" they had cried at the swimming meet there the year before. "Viva, Fish!"
She bent forward. Her arms were stretched back behind her. Then she dived into the water. She swam at just the right speed. It would be fast enough to keep her close to the leaders during the Olympic trials. But it would not be too fast. At the end of the race, she would still have some strength left for that last push. She would pass the others—right near the end— and win as she had in Mexico City.

Viva, Fish!

It was much later when she touched the pool wall after the last lap. How long had she been swimming? She wiped the water from her eyes and looked through the glass that ringed the pool. It was dark outside. She had lost track of the time. She had also lost track of how far she had swum. It must have been more than 1500 meters.

Jan shook her head. It was not like her to lose track of things while swimming. But there had been something worrying her. Something about the Olympic trials. It was something she had not told anyone.

CHAPTER 3

Sorry

The red letters on the sign danced on and off. *Sal's Pizza House. Sal's Pizza House.* When Jan walked under the sign and through the door, she saw Marty and the others waiting for her.

"What took you so long?" a swimmer named Nancy Harris asked. Her blonde hair looked wild and stiff from too much pool water. "It's almost 7:30!"

"Leave her alone," Marty broke in. "I'm sure Fish had a good reason."

Jan sat down and smiled weakly. "I just lost track of the time," she said.

"Don't worry about it," Marty told her. "We saved you some pizza."

"It was better a half hour ago," Nancy Harris said with a laugh.

Jan took a bite of the cold pizza. "It's fine," she said. She looked at Marty, who smiled.

"We were just talking about Shirley Ford," a woman named Maria Johnson said. "She's in all the papers. Have you been reading about her, Jan?"

The bite of pizza caught in Jan's throat. "Sure," she said after a few seconds. "Who hasn't?"

Nancy Harris smiled like a hungry animal about to strike. "Yesterday, Shirley Ford swam the best 1500 ever."

"I read that story," Jan said.

Marty reached over to give Jan's shoulder a pat. "That was just practice," she told her. "The trials are all that matter."

"Yes, but Shirley Ford swims the 100-meter as well," Nancy Harris went on. "Jan will have to beat her twice."

"What are you trying to do?" Jan asked, jumping up. "Make me worry? Shirley Ford doesn't worry me. Shirley Ford won't beat me. The only one who can beat me is *me!*"

Jan finished the piece of pizza and pushed away from the table to get a Coke. The last thing that she wanted to do just then was to talk about Shirley Ford. She was worried about the young swimmer—that was the secret she had been keeping. Shirley Ford was only 16—several years younger than Jan. But Shirley was already one of the best swimmers in the country. She was sure to give Jan a run for her money in the Olympic trials.

Shirley Ford was still on Jan's mind when it happened. As she headed back to the table with her Coke, something knocked her feet out from under her. She kept herself from falling. But the drink spilled all over her.

"Oh, I'm sorry." A young man quickly got up from a table by the window. "I wasn't thinking. I mean, I was thinking. I mean, I was looking out the window just now. There's an island out there. My feet must have been in the way."

He started to dry Jan's arm off with some paper napkins. But Jan grabbed them away from him and did it herself.

"I'm really sorry," the man said again.

"Forget it," Jan told him. "It doesn't matter. I'm used to being wet."

"Well, can I get you another drink?"

"No. It's OK." Jan looked up as she put the napkins on the table. "Why are you smiling?" she asked. "It's not that funny. Or am I supposed to know you or something?"

"Well, we met—sort of. I'm a swimmer too. My name is Jeff Nakamura. We met this afternoon at the water fountain."

"Oh, yeah. I remember you. It's hard to get a drink with you around."

"I was really thirsty, but I got a little angry about it. I tried to tell you I was sorry later on, but your coach kicked me out."

"Oh." Jan smiled quickly. "Well." Then she looked across the room. "Listen," she said.

"You must have better things to do than talk to me."

Jeff started to say something, but Jan saw Marty waving to her. She and the others were getting up from the table.

"I have to leave," Jan said, cutting Jeff off. "My friends are going." She started to walk away.

"Well, it was nice bumping into you," Jeff called after her.

The words stopped Jan for a second. She turned and looked at him.

"You're crazy," she said.

"Well, you know what I mean," Jeff said. "And I'm sorry about—"

But Jan didn't hear the rest of what Jeff said. She was already at the other end of Sal's Pizza House.

Mile Island 4

Jeff Nakamura stood outside Sal's, watching the red taillights of the cars going back to town grow small. When they went out of sight, the night grew very dark.

It was also growing cold. Jeff thought about putting on his sweatsuit top. But he didn't. He didn't get on his Honda, either.

Instead, he did something strange. He ran down some stone steps to the empty beach. Then he started taking off his clothes. First his shirt. Then his shoes. Soon he stood there in just his shorts.

He could just see the tops of the waves. They were hitting the beach 20 yards in front of him. He couldn't see the island. But he knew it was there—somewhere out there in the dark, a little more than a mile out to sea.

All of a sudden, Jeff threw his arms in the air. He gave a wild call and started running toward the waves.

He ran into the water. It was as cold as ice. Jeff started swimming slowly, out away from the beach.

He ducked under the first few waves. Then his strong arms took him past the waves, out where the water rose and fell slowly around him.

On and on Jeff swam through the dark ocean. It was black all around him. There was no moon to show him the way. But he didn't need to see. Somehow he knew where he should go.

Again and again, his arms dug into the black water. His legs kicked hard. Then, finally, a black shape far ahead of him stood up from the water. It was Mile Island. The place where he was heading.

Jeff pushed forward even harder. But soon his arms and legs began to hurt. And then the sea began to fight him. For every inch Jeff moved forward, the sea pushed him back two more. The water rose in angry mountains all around him.

Then it happened. It was only a tiny wave. Jeff should have been able to swim through it or over it. But he was too tired. The wave smashed into his face. Jeff could feel the burning salt water rushing down his throat.

He coughed and fought the water. All of his training was forgotten. He splashed wildly as another wave broke over him. The ocean seemed to be pushing him down.

Stop it, he told himself. Take it easy. He forced himself to take a deep breath, and then he tried to float. The waves kept pushing, but he let them push him now—back toward the beach.

At last Jeff saw the lights from Sal's Pizza House again. With the little energy that he had left, he started to swim. Soon he could hear the sound of water crashing onto the beach. Then he was free from the ocean. He dragged himself toward his clothes and threw himself down on the cold sand.

"Maybe she's right," he said to himself with a small laugh. "Maybe I am crazy."

Then he sat on the beach for a long time without laughing. Something hurt deep inside him. And Jeff knew what it was. He had not made it to Mile Island. But he knew it wouldn't be his last try.

CHAPTER 5

In the News

The news hit Jan like a sharp blow. She looked hard at Nancy Harris.

"It can't be," Jan said. "You must have heard it wrong."

"No way," Nancy Harris answered. "I heard it straight from Coach Hooper. Shirley Ford is joining our team in a few weeks. I know it's true. We have the best women's swim team in the country here at Los Alamos. It seems only right for Shirley Ford to be part of it."

"Well, I don't like it," Jan said. She pushed her hair into the swimming cap and got on the starting block.

"Don't worry about it, Fish." Marty was looking up at Jan. "I'll bet Shirley Ford just wants a chance to train with you. Then she can study what it is that makes you so good."

"You mean she can study how to beat me." Jan dived into the pool and started swimming. Right away she felt better. Swimming always made her troubles go away.

She swam the first 50 meters fast. Then she brought up her knees, did a flip turn, and came racing back. She pushed hard all the way. When she got out, Coach Hooper was waiting with the stopwatch.

"That last 50 was great," Hooper said. "You keep that up and no one will be able to beat you."

"No one?" Jan asked.

"No one," Hooper said. "Not even Shirley Ford."

Jan smiled.

That was when Marty walked up with the television reporter. As soon as Jan saw him, she knew she didn't like him. Every hair on his head was right where it belonged. And each bright white tooth was just where it should be too. The man's smile was almost too bright to look at. It was pointed right at Jan.

"Well," the man said. "Here she is right now." He held out his hand to Jan. "I sure am pleased to meet you, Ms. Fisher."

"That's the Fish, all right," Marty said to him. Jan thought that Marty sounded silly.

"My name is Kurt Maxwell," the smiling teeth went on. "Can I call you Jan?"

"I guess so," Jan said. "Why not?" She looked away.

"Jan, I'd like to ask you a few questions. You're big news, you know."

Jan saw the second man then. He was pointing a TV camera at her. A bright light went on in her face. She held up a hand to cover her eyes.

Kurt Maxwell laughed a laugh that didn't sound real. "Don't worry about that!" he said. "You'll get used to the light. Now come on. Come stand over here with me. I want the pool behind us in the picture."

"Go ahead, Fish," Marty said, pushing her along. "Tell them you're the best."

Jan took her place beside Kurt Maxwell. She didn't want to do it, but she stood there anyway. Then she felt the reporter's large hand on her shoulder. His arm was around her. The camera was rolling.

"This is Kurt Maxwell speaking to you from the Los Alamos pool. Many young swimmers are training here for the Olympic trials that will be held in just nine weeks. Some of these swimmers will go on to the Olympics. One who I'm sure will go has a name we all know. She won one gold and one silver medal at the Olympics almost four years ago. And she was the star of last year's swimming meet in Mexico City. Of course, I'm talking about Jan 'The Fish' Fisher. Jan, how is your training going at Los Alamos?"

Jan looked at the camera and somehow the words just came out. She could always talk about swimming. "Fine, Kurt. I'm sure you know that this is one of the best pools in the country. There are lots of great swimmers training here. There's—" She fought to keep from saying Shirley Ford. What she did say surprised even Jan. "There's Jeff Nakamura, Andy Nakamura's younger brother."

"No kidding!" Kurt Maxwell laughed another empty laugh. "The brother of the great swimming star Andy Nakamura?"

Then Maxwell turned away from the camera. His blue eyes looked straight into Jan's brown ones. His smile seemed as bright as the television light.

"That's an interesting fact. But tell us about the Fish. How will you do in the Olympics? Can we look forward to seeing some new world records?"

"Well, first things first," Jan said. "First there are the trials. Then the Olympics. I'm sure many records will be set there. I just hope I set one or two myself."

"Well, I'm sure you're America's favorite, Jan. All of us will be pulling for you."

"Thank you."

"Thank you, Jan Fisher. For Channel 12 News, this is Kurt Maxwell at the Los Alamos pool."

The camera light went off. Kurt Maxwell's smile stayed on. "Did you get my good side?" Maxwell asked the man with the camera.

The other man nodded. Then he walked away. The door shut behind him, and he was gone.

Kurt Maxwell let go of Jan Fisher's shoulder then. The marks from his fingers stayed behind on her skin.

"Say, you were great!" he told Jan. "Let's do it again some other time." With his smile still flashing, Kurt Maxwell turned toward Marty. "Thanks for finding her," he said.

Then, like the man with the camera, he was gone.

Jan looked at Marty. "Was that guy for real?" Jan asked.

"I know what you mean," Marty said. "But it's important for you to be on TV. More people will know how really great you are."

Out of Reach 6.

Jeff broke some eggs into a pan and started cooking them. In the next room, the TV news was on. But Jeff wasn't really listening. He had other things on his mind.

Practice that day had gone well. Jeff's time for the 1500 was better than it had ever been before. And he had felt strong at the finish.

. . . Jan "The Fish" Fisher. Jan, how is your training. . . .

He was really happy. Practice was like a dream come true. He had almost called home to tell his parents. For the first time, he was almost sure he would make the Olympic team.

. . . Jeff Nakamura, Andy Nakamura's younger brother.

28

The words from the television suddenly caught Jeff's ear. He ran into the next room so that he could see the set. To his surprise, he saw that the words had come from Jan Fisher. Now the reporter was talking.

No kidding! The brother of the great swimming star Andy Nakamura?

Jeff couldn't believe what he had heard. He stood listening until the story was over. He was still standing there when the On-the-Spot News music came on. There were loud horns and beating drums—enough noise to make even the silliest story sound important. When a picture of a new kind of stove to buy came on, Jeff remembered that he was hungry. He could almost smell the meat in the TV picture cooking.

The eggs! They were brown and turning black when Jeff made it back into the kitchen. The room was beginning to fill with smoke. Making a face, Jeff put the pan in the sink and covered it with cold water.

A minute later he was on the telephone, calling the number the Los Alamos swim team list had next to Jan Fisher's name.

Someone else answered, but soon Jan came on the line.

"Listen," Jeff said. "I just burned my eggs. Would you like to go out to dinner?"

"What? Who is this?"

"Oh, I'm sorry. This is Jeff Nakamura."

"Who?"

"Jeff Nakamura—you know, Andy Nakamura's brother," Jeff said. "You were just talking about me on TV."

Now Jan's voice sounded different. "No kidding? You mean they really put that stuff on the air?"

"They sure did," Jeff told her. Then he found himself talking very fast. About swimming. About dinner. About Mile Island. He was talking so fast he almost missed Jan's answer.

"What was that?" he said. "Did you say something?"

"I said OK," Jan said. "I'll go to dinner with you. I forgot to buy groceries. Where should we meet?"

"I'll pick you up," Jeff said. "Just tell me where you live."

Jan lived in a room at the back of a large house owned by a woman named Blake. Mrs. Blake had a kind face that broke into a smile when she saw Jeff.

"You must be Jeff," she said as she took his hand. "It's so nice to meet one of Jan's friends at last. I'll go get her."

In a moment Jeff could hear their voices in the hall.

"Don't you want to change, dear?" Mrs. Blake was saying.

Then there was Jan's voice. "I'm only going out with Jeff Nakamura," she said.

Jan held on tightly as Jeff's Honda went over the bumpy roads to the beach. On the way Jeff pointed out the building where he lived. It was red and white, with a large palm tree in front.

There were no palm trees in front of Sal's Pizza House. There was only the sign with its dancing letters and a few cars in the big lot. Jeff parked the Honda, and the two swimmers went inside.

After they had ordered and found a place to sit, Jan looked out the window. "Is that the island that you were talking about before?"

Jeff looked outside. It had been a clear day, and the blue sky was still bright. Waves rose and fell. Mile Island looked close enough to touch.

"That's the one," Jeff said.

Jan looked at the small spot of land. "Why is it so important to you?"

"I can't really say for sure," Jeff said. "It's just that it's a long, hard swim. If I make it to the Olympics, everyone will know I'm as good a swimmer as my brother. But even if I only make it to Mile Island, at least I'll know it."

Jan nodded. "I don't have any brothers or sisters," she said. "But I see what you mean. If you could swim out to that island, it would really prove something."

Jeff nodded. He watched her as he ate. Then he asked a question that had been on his mind. "How did you know I was Andy Nakamura's brother?"

"That's easy," Jan said. She looked down. "I asked. Besides, I eat, drink, and sleep swimming. So of course I know about all of Andy's records. Swimming is all there is in my life."

Jeff found that hard to believe. But when he told Jan that, she got angry.

"Look at me," she said. "What else could there be?"

Jeff found himself looking into the same angry face he had seen at the water fountain. He saw much more than a great swimmer, but he couldn't find the words to say what he was thinking.

"Boy, you really are something!" Jan exploded. "You don't even know when to lie!"

"I'm sorry," Jeff said. And he said it again later when they were outside Sal's Pizza House.

"You're crazy," Jan said. "And will you stop saying you're sorry? I just lose my head like that sometimes."

Jeff forced a smile. He searched for something to say. "So swimming is your whole life?" he asked at last.

"Pretty much. It does something to me that nothing else can," Jan said. "The water makes me feel good. If I don't feel good, all I have to do is go down to the pool. If I'm sick, working out in the pool makes me feel better."

Something about the way Jan spoke made Jeff feel close to her for the first time. He reached out to touch her arm. But Jan backed away.

"I don't feel that way about you," she said. She started walking toward the parking lot. Jeff followed, but he didn't know what to think. Jan Fisher seemed as hard to reach as Mile Island.

CHAPTER 7

New Member for the Team

Coach Hooper's tin-can voice rang out above the other noises at the pool.

"Jan, come here. There's someone I want you to meet."

Coach Hooper was standing next to a girl in a bright blue swimsuit. The girl was tall, with long, strong arms and legs. She looked like a machine built for swimming, but she had the face of a child. She looked just like her pictures.

"Hello," she said, holding out her hand as Jan came up. "My name is Shirley Ford."

"Pleased to meet you." The words came out of Jan's mouth before she knew what had happened. She shook Shirley Ford's hand. The young swimmer smiled.

"I want you two to work together," Coach Hooper said. "I think you two are the best hope the Los Alamos team has for the Olympic trials. And the trials are only four weeks away now. If you work together, you'll learn a lot from each other."

"Oh, I'm sure I can learn a lot from Jan," Shirley Ford said.

Coach Hooper waited for Jan's answer. Jan just nodded. Inside her, something wanted to cry out, *No! I won't do it! It isn't fair! How can you ask me to help her beat me?* But she didn't say it. She just kept nodding. She had been feeling a little sick all week long. She was probably catching a bad cold. The idea of helping Shirley Ford made her feel even worse.

"Why don't we start out with the 100-meter freestyle?" Coach Hooper said. "Women—on your blocks."

Jan, Shirley Ford, Nancy Harris, and two others got up on the blocks. They bent forward with their arms out behind them. Then, at the sound of the whistle, they hit the water.

The race was on. Jan quickly pulled away from Nancy Harris and the others. But Shirley Ford stayed right with her, stroke for stroke, down the pool. On every third stroke, Jan turned her head for air. First to the right, then three strokes later to the left. Each time she turned her head to the left, she saw Shirley Ford—still next to her.

At the far end of the pool, Jan turned with a quick flip and then pushed off. When she came up for the first stroke, she found herself half a body length in front of Shirley Ford. The two of them stayed that way until the end of the race. Jan Fisher finished in first place. Shirley Ford was second. The rest were far behind.

When they got out of the water, Shirley Ford couldn't wait to talk to Jan. "What did you do on the turn?" she asked. "You really left me behind."

Jan smiled. "That's a little secret of mine," she said.

Shirley Ford just shook her head. "I'll have to watch you really close to learn how to do that!"

Then Shirley Ford walked away, bright and full of life. She started talking to one of the other swimmers.

Jan sat down by herself, wondering what was wrong. She had never felt so tired after swimming a 100-meter race before. Her head was pounding.

The last thing she needed was Marty's news. "Fish, you'll never guess what!" Marty said, running up to her.

Jan didn't have to guess. Before she could say a word, Kurt Maxwell was in front of her with his perfect teeth, his hot light, and his TV camera.

"I don't feel like talking right now," Jan said. She started to stand up.

"Hey, listen," Kurt Maxwell said, not listening to her at all. "You're news. The people out there are eating up stories about Jan Fisher. And they're hungry for more."

"You make me sound like a hamburger."

Maxwell flashed his bright smile. "Come on. You *are* like a hamburger to your fans—but a very special kind of hamburger. Don't let it turn you off just because they want you." He looked at Jan with soft, big eyes. "Come on," he said. "Just a minute of your time?"

Jan was too tired to fight. She nodded. "OK," she said at last. "But for just a minute."

The bright light went on. The film in the camera started rolling. Kurt Maxwell's voice started putting words together in that perfect way he had of talking.

"This is Kurt Maxwell speaking to you from the Los Alamos pool. I'm talking with Jan Fisher—a fine young swimmer who is training for the Olympic trials. Just today another fine young swimmer joined the Los Alamos team—Shirley Ford. Jan, can you tell us how you feel about Shirley Ford coming to Los Alamos?"

CHAPTER

In Hot Water 8

The telephone rang. Jeff woke up with a start. At first, he didn't know what was happening. He reached out in the dark and knocked over a lamp. At last he found the phone.

"This is Mrs. Blake," the voice on the other end of the line said.

Jeff turned on the light and looked at the clock. It was two o'clock in the morning. "Mrs. *Who?*"

"Mrs. Blake," the voice on the other end said. "The Mrs. Blake that Jan lives with. I'm sorry to wake you up. But I need your help, Jeff. I need your help right away."

* * *

When Jeff got there, Mrs. Blake looked worried.

40

"At first I didn't know what to do," she told Jeff. "Then I thought of you. You're the only friend who has ever come here to see Jan. I thought maybe you could help."

"What's the matter?" Jeff asked. "Has Jan been hurt?"

"I don't know," Mrs. Blake said as she led Jeff through the house. "She's been sick this last week—very sick. But she keeps acting as if nothing is wrong. You know how she is. I don't think she wants anyone to know she's sick. But tonight she was worse. She had a bad cough and a fever. So I forced her to take something for them and to go to bed early."

They were at the end of the hall now. Mrs. Blake reached to open the door to Jan's room.

"Then I woke up in the middle of the night," Mrs. Blake explained. "It was like when my children were sick. I suppose I was worried about Jan." She let the door swing open.

Jeff followed her into the room. It was a mess. Everywhere there were magazines about swimming. Old, yellowed news stories were pinned to the wall. There were dirty clothes all over the floor. Only one small table in the corner was clean. On it were medals and prizes Jan had won for swimming. In the middle of them were the Olympic silver and gold.

Jeff turned to the bed. It was empty. Jan wasn't in sight. Jeff turned to Mrs. Blake for an answer.

The woman was shaking her head and holding on to the door. "She's gone. She was gone when I came to check on her. Her car was gone too. And she left the front door wide open. What could have happened? When that girl gets an idea in her head. . . ."

"I know," Jeff said, still looking around the room. "She can act a little cr—" He stopped. "But she's sick?"

"She's very sick," Mrs. Blake told him. "I'm sure she has a fever. I keep thinking maybe she wasn't right in the head. Why would she just walk out in the middle of the night? Where would she go?"

Jeff's eyes came to a stop at a pile of magazines. The top one was opened to a story about Jan Fisher. Across the page were the words *I Love the Water*.

The words made Jeff think. He remembered standing next to Jan that other night outside

Sal's Pizza House. He remembered the look on her face. Her words came back to him.

"I know one place she might be," Jeff told Mrs. Blake. "You stay by the telephone in case she calls. If I find out anything, I'll call you."

* * *

The air was cold as Jeff raced his Honda down the dark streets to the Los Alamos Swim Club. When he got there, he could see that the lights in Pool Number Two were on. At the door he found a set of keys still hanging from the lock.

Jeff opened the door and ran down the hall to the pool. As he swung open the second door, he could hear the sound of someone in the water.

"Jan!" he called, but the person in the pool kept on swimming.

"Jan!" he called again. But she swam on and on—like a machine. Down to the far end of the pool. Back up again. Then down. Then back. On and on she swam, not hearing his voice, not missing a stroke.

She must be fine, Jeff thought. Then he saw that Jan was having trouble. She wasn't swimming straight. She was moving across the lane and bumping into the rope.

Jeff kicked off his shoes. He jumped into the water and swam after her. He caught her near the far wall and pulled her up. There was a wild look in her eyes. But to Jeff's surprise, she didn't fight him. Instead she closed her eyes and passed out.

Even in the water, Jeff could feel the heat of her body. She was burning up with fever.

CHAPTER 9
The Trials

Almost everyone laughed. They had all been training hard and worrying about how the team would do ever since Jan went into the hospital. They needed something to make them laugh again. So when they saw Jeff walking out to the pool, almost everyone laughed.

Jeff did look strange. He had shaved his head and his whole body. Some swimmers believed that shaving the body helped a person swim faster.

"Do well in the Olympics and maybe some company can use you to sell razors," one person joked.

Marty didn't laugh. "Why don't you leave him alone?" she shouted at the others. They

45

stopped laughing and walked away when they saw her angry face. Then Marty turned to Jeff. "They shouldn't do that. And I shouldn't have been so hard on you before, either. I was trying to help Jan. But if it hadn't been for you a few weeks ago, Jan. . . ." Marty didn't finish the sentence.

"I know," Jeff said.

Jan had been in the hospital for three weeks. Then she had spent a week at home. She was supposed to come back to the pool that day.

Everyone had been waiting for that day. But not just because of Jan. That Monday was the first day of the Olympic trials, and the first of the men's races would be held in just a short time. The first of the women's races would start on Tuesday.

"Oh, man. You're a sight!"

The voice caught Jeff by surprise. He turned to see Jan Fisher standing behind him. She was wearing the same bright red sweatsuit she always did. But she looked thin and tired. She smiled, but it was a strange smile.

"You're still crazy," she said.

All Jeff did was smile back.

"Fish!" cried Marty. "How are you?"

"Afraid," Jan answered. "I haven't done any swimming for so long." She looked at the pool as if it might bite her. Then she looked up quickly. "Do you race today?" she asked Jeff.

"Yeah," he said. "In the big one—1500 meters."

"Well, good luck," Jan told him.

Jeff laughed. "Thanks, but I may need more than luck. I've tried everything I can think of already." He ran a hand over his shiny head.

"Well, try this," Jan said and whispered something in his ear.

"Do you really think that will help?" Jeff asked. He looked a little surprised.

"Just try it," Jan told him.

"OK. I will. Will you be there to watch?"

"Sure," Jan said. "I'll be there."

* * *

When Coach Hooper saw Jan, she wanted to talk to her in her office.

"I'm glad you're back," Hooper said. "How are you feeling?"

"Great," Jan said. She tried to look very happy.

"Well, you look tired," Hooper said. She kept looking hard at Jan and didn't speak for a moment. "Jan, I won't play games," she said at last. "You and I have been working together for more than a year. We both know that no one can be as sick as you've been and stay a strong swimmer."

Jan started to say something, but Coach Hooper held up her hand.

"Listen for a minute," she said. "I just don't think you'll have enough power and speed for both of your races. But maybe you'll have enough for one. I think you should swim in just one."

Hooper sat back in her chair and waited for Jan to say something. But no words came to Jan. She could hear the clock on the wall.

"The 1500-meter freestyle is tomorrow morning," Hooper went on after a while. "I think it will be too much for you. I think you should forget about it. Rest, and then try the 100-meter tomorrow afternoon." She reached out and took Jan's hand. "I think it's the best shot you have."

"OK," Jan said after a moment. Her voice was so soft Meg Hooper almost didn't hear it.

"Good," said Hooper. She was all business again. "Now get ready. There's a practice for the 100-meter in five minutes."

The water felt good to Jan as she swam the 100-meter practice. It was as if she had not been gone. She had to try harder, but still she swam well. She and Shirley Ford stayed even through the whole race. Then they touched the pool wall at the same time.

It was there that the tie ended. Shirley Ford jumped out of the pool. Jan hung on to the pool wall, trying to catch her breath. When she climbed out, she was still tired. Marty ran up with a towel.

"Come on, Fish!" Marty said. "We have to hurry if we want to see Jeff's race."

"Go on without me," Jan said.

"Fish! You told him you'd be there."

"Go on without me!" Jan shouted. "Just leave me alone!"

* * *

Marty sat by herself in the stands. Jeff saw her and nodded. Then he and the other swimmers got on the blocks. The starter lifted the gun to start the race.

Suddenly Jeff called out. "Wait a minute!"

As everyone watched, he reached down to his swimsuit. He checked the strings to make sure the suit was on tight.

"OK," Jeff said. "Ready."

Now the other swimmers looked down at their suits. But the gun went off at the very same time. Jeff hit the water fast.

CHAPTER 10
The Race

"Good luck, Jan."

Jan looked down at the hand in front of her. She looked at the person who was holding it out. Then she reached out and shook it.

"Thanks," she said. "Good luck to you too, Shirley."

She watched Shirley Ford walk away. Then she pushed her hair up into her swimming cap. She started toward the blocks. It was almost time for the finals in the women's 100-meter race.

"You can shake my hand too," someone behind her said.

Jan turned. "Hello, Jeff." Then her eyes opened wide. "Do you mean you made the team?"

Jeff nodded. "I came in third in my race."

Jan smiled. She knew that the top three swimmers in the finals for each race made the team. "I'll bet shaving your body helped," she told him.

"What really helped was your trick," said Jeff. "I picked up a second on each of the other swimmers while they worried about their suits falling off."

Jeff smiled, but he stopped when he saw the worried look on Jan's face. "Well, your friend Marty made the team too," he went on. "Where is she, anyway? I thought she'd be here."

Jan shook her head. "I don't know," she said. "I think she's mad at me because I missed your race. I thought you'd be mad too."

"Oh, it's OK," Jeff said. He watched Jan climb up on the block. "But I wouldn't miss *this* race for the world."

"You're crazy," Jan said. She looked back at the tall, thin man with the bald head.

Jeff smiled. "Kiss for luck?"

"Come off it!" Jan said sharply.

"Oh," said Jeff. "I'm sor—"

Jan cut him off. "Don't say it," she said. "Just cheer for me when the race starts."

"I will," said Jeff. "You just win."

Jan smiled a weak smile. Then she turned to look at the other swimmers on the blocks. There were seven of them. But Jan saw only Shirley Ford.

In a moment the starter lifted the gun. Jan bent forward with her arms out behind her. Her mind raced.

The gun went off. Jan shot out over the water, then down. She came up swimming, dead even with Shirley Ford. The other swimmers were all half a body length behind them.

She swam hard. Every three strokes, Jan turned her head for air. Every six strokes, she could see to her left. Each time she looked, she saw the same thing. Shirley Ford was still beside her. Shirley Ford was matching her, stroke for stroke.

The far wall was coming up fast. Jan knew that she had to beat Shirley Ford on the turn, as she had so often in practice. She reached out to touch the wall at the same time as Shirley Ford. She pulled her head down and under. Her legs folded against her chest. Around she went. She pushed off. It was a good turn. As she came up for air, she looked to her right. She was still dead even with Shirley Ford.

Then it happened. Slowly, as if in a bad dream, Shirley Ford started to pull away. Jan fought to go faster, but her body seemed heavy in the water. Shirley Ford was still pulling away. And now Nancy Harris was coming up from behind.

Jan reached for more—the way she had often reached for more energy or speed in other races. But this time there was nothing left. Nancy Harris passed her, and then another swimmer moved by. When Jan touched the pool wall, she had finished fourth.

CHAPTER 11

Water to Cross

The people were all around her. But Jan wanted nothing to do with them. She didn't want to hear what they were saying.

"Jan, I'm sorry."

"Jan, I never thought that—"

Worst of all was Kurt Maxwell with his television news. "Jan, can you tell us how you feel after losing so badly?"

"Just get off my back!"

Jan pushed past Maxwell and stormed out the door. Coach Hooper's tin-can voice rang out behind her. Jeff and Marty were calling too. But Jan wouldn't listen. She had to get away.

She didn't stop even when she got to her car. She started the engine and pushed the gas pedal to the floor. The car went racing down the street, moving faster and faster. Suddenly a horn sounded. Jan had to turn the wheel quickly to keep from hitting a car coming toward her. The tires screamed. Her car went around the corner on two wheels.

She wiped at her eyes. She thought she could see someone crossing the street, but she didn't care. The person jumped back out of the way as the car raced by.

Fourth place!

Jan pressed down on the gas pedal even harder. She turned this way and that. She was too angry to think where she was going. Soon she had no idea where she was. It was all she could do to keep the car on the road.

When she stopped the car at last, she found herself at the beach. The tears had stopped. But she had a sick feeling deep inside. Jan looked down the street. Sal's Pizza House sat quietly on the sand. Looking close enough to touch, Mile Island sat quietly on the sea.

Mile Island. Jeff Nakamura's island. Jan remembered the look on Jeff's face when he had told her about it. Then her own words

about the island came back to her. It was as if she had just said them. *If you could swim out to that island, it would really prove something.*

She was out of the car and running. Then she was in the water, swimming. A sad and angry feeling drove her on. It drove her past the big waves and on out to sea.

Her arms and legs were not as strong as they had been. But the feeling inside her kept her going. Again and again, her arms cut into the water. Again and again the ocean tried to push her back. But she fought hard, pounding the water with angry kicks. She didn't stop fighting until a long time later—when she climbed onto the brown rocks of Mile Island. She had made the swim.

Jan sat on the rocks a long time—just thinking. After a while, some things seemed clear. Swimming had become too important in her life. When she didn't win the race, it had seemed as if her life were over. Because, as she had said, swimming *was* her life. She had become the Fish. She was not Jan Fisher anymore. She had shut people out. Things would have to change now. But she wondered if she could remember how to be Jan Fisher.

She was still sitting on the rocks when the sun went down. She had raced the 100-meter finals over and over in her mind. And she knew that it was OK to have lost the race. She had done her best, and that was what mattered. Besides, since she had come in fourth, she would still go to the Olympics. Finishing fourth made her a part of the relay team. She would go to the Games with all the others. Marty. Nancy Harris. Shirley Ford. Jeff Nakamura.

Jeff! She had made his swim to Mile Island. But as she stood up to leave, she knew that she would never tell him.

* * *

After the long swim back to the beach, Jan tried to call Jeff. There was no answer on the telephone. She decided to drive past the red and white building anyway. The tall, thin palm tree stood there looking sad. All the lights in Jeff's place were out. His Honda wasn't in sight.

Somehow Jan knew that Jeff would be at the swim club. When she saw the Honda parked outside, she started looking for him the way he had once looked for her. She went from room to room inside the building.

She was coming out of Pool Number Two when she saw him at last. His bald head was bent down over the water fountain. He looked hot and tired. He was taking a long, cool drink. He didn't hear her coming up behind him. He didn't even know she was there until she put her hand on his shoulder.

"Hey," she said. "Other people want a drink too."

A surprised Jeff turned around, then smiled.

Jan smiled back. "Come on with me," she said. "I'll buy you a Coke."